This book
belongs to

....

To Rosalie

FREDERICK WARNE

Published by the Penguin Group
Penguin Books Ltd, 80 Strand, London WC2R 0RL, England
Penguin Young Readers Group, 345 Hudson Street,
New York, New York 10014, U.S.A.
Penguin Books Australia Ltd, 250 Camberwell Road, Camberwell,
Victoria 3124, Australia
Canada, India, New Zealand, South Africa

1 3 5 7 9 10 8 6 4 2

ISBN-13: 978 07232 5827 8
ISBN-10: 0 7232 5827 9

Printed in Great Britain

Rose's Special Secret

by Kay Woodward

Welcome to the Flower Fairy Garden!

Where are the fairies?
Where can we find them?
We've seen the fairy-rings
They leave behind them!

Is it a secret
No one is telling?
Why, in your garden
Surely they're dwelling!

No need for journeying,
Seeking afar:
Where there are flowers,
There fairies are!

Contents

Chapter One
A Narrow Escape

"I'll miss you," Rose whispered softly. The Flower Fairy looked at the tangle of thorns and withered leaves for the very last time. For as long as she could remember, this tatty, overgrown, *wonderful* rosebush had been her home. She'd trimmed and tended its crooked stems, encouraging the ancient plant to send out delicate pink buds every spring and summer. She'd done everything in her power

to take care of it. And in return, the prickly plant had given her soft pink petals to wear and a beautiful place to live. But disaster was approaching—and not even fairy dust could save the rosebush now.

A loud *swoosh* interrupted Rose's

melancholy thoughts, and she glanced up as a sparrow hurtled past, chirping noisily. When she heard what the anxious bird had to say, Rose hastily flung her leafy bag over one shoulder. *They* were on their way. It was time for *her* to go.

"Good-bye," said Rose, a lone tear

trickling down her cheek. "I'll never forget you."

As if saying farewell, the rosebush waved in the breeze.

Feeling that her heart might break, the Flower Fairy gave a brief watery smile, took a deep breath, and then fluttered to the ground. She landed nimbly on dainty feet and hurried in the direction of the morning sun, which was already casting a golden glow over the leafy wilderness that lay before her. As she dodged around weeds and leaped over rocks, Rose's mind whirred.

It had been less than a week since the dreadful rumors had invaded the overgrown garden. The bees had started it, buzzing odd-sounding new words: *Decking. Concrete. Patio.* No one knew what they meant, but they sounded mean, dangerous, and very scary.

Then the human intruders came. They stomped through the garden, crushing delicate flowers and forging wide, muddy pathways with their enormous boots, even uprooting entire plants that had the misfortune to block their way.

Rose and her Flower Fairy friends could no longer hop and flutter freely from flower to flower—they now seemed to spend most of their time scurrying between one leafy plant and the next. They knew, as every Flower Fairy knows, that the only way to make sure that Flower Fairyland remained truly safe was by keeping it very, very secret. The only problem was, their precious homes were disappearing fast—and they were running out of places to hide.

"What are we going to *do*?" Rose cried helplessly to Dandelion. He was one of the toughest, most resourceful Flower Fairies she knew—as well as one of the most brightly dressed. If anyone knew how to deal with these troublesome humans, he would.

"*Do*? Oh, there's nothing we can *do*," Dandelion said matter-of-factly. He swung from one tall rose stem to another, his beautiful yellow-and-black wings almost dazzling Rose with their brilliance. "I've seen it all before. They come. They weed and rake and sow. They roll out carpets of green grass. And then they go. Before long, you have a lovely wilderness once more.'

"But where shall we *go?*" Rose said, her voice trembling. She was trying desperately not to cry, even though everything sounded pretty hopeless.

"It's all right for me," said Dandelion, smoothing down his jaunty yellow-and-green outfit. "It doesn't matter how many times they pull up my flower—it will always grow again. And I'm a bit of a wanderer at heart! But rosebushes..." He scratched his head, noticing for perhaps the first time that Rose didn't share his happy-go-lucky mood. "Well ... if I were you, I'd take a holiday," he suggested kindly. "Go and see a bit of Flower Fairyland. Meet some new Flower Fairies. You might find another rosebush—one even better than this one."

"I'll *never* find a better home than this!" exclaimed Rose. But deep down, she knew that Dandelion was right. Her beloved rosebush wasn't safe any more—and no matter how much she disliked the idea of moving, she *had* to go.

Now, as she rushed toward safety, the tiny Flower Fairy thought she heard the distant sound of metal crunching into dry, cracked earth. Her steps quickened. In no time, she reached the crumbly bricks—covered with masses of pink and peach and lilac blooms— that marked the edge of the world she knew.

Rose looked up and up ... and up. She'd

been this way once before, but somehow, she didn't remember the wall being quite this high. It towered above her, the top so far away that it was almost out of sight.

Rose flopped down onto a nearby mushroom, resting the bag on her knee. Inside, she'd carefully stowed all her possessions: the petal dress that she kept for best, a sunny yellow flower that Dandelion had given her as a going-away present (he said that it would make an excellent umbrella), a single pink rosebud to remind her of her old home, and a tiny gossamer bag of fairy dust. This last item had to be saved for emergencies. But as she peered up at the lofty wall, Rose realized that she would need all her fairy dust to help her fly over this—the very first obstacle that she'd encountered. Once her fairy dust was gone, what would she do *then* for fairy magic? She could make no more fairy dust until she found another rosebush.

"I say," said a soft voice, "you're looking terribly sad. Is there anything I can do to help?"

Rose brushed blonde curls from her eyes and examined the wall more closely. A Flower Fairy was watching her curiously from among gently ruffled pink petals. It was Sweet Pea! She wore a delicate

pink skirt made from layers of the same petals as her flower, and a leaf-green bodice. Her hair was long, dark, and wavy.

"Because if you're wondering about climbing this wall, you needn't worry," Sweet Pea went on. "It's a snap. No need for even the tiniest pinch of fairy dust."

And Rose saw that it was true. The entire wall was covered with curly, green tendrils—ideal handholds and footholds for fairy feet. She grinned widely at the helpful Flower Fairy and picked up her bag once more.

"Come on," said Sweet Pea brightly. "I'll show you the way."

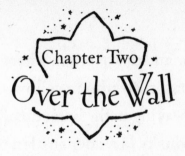

Chapter Two
Over the Wall

"Oooh . . ." breathed Rose. She'd never seen anything like it—ever. From her bird's-eye perch on top of the old wall, she gazed at a whole new world that stretched far into the distance. It looked utterly magical.

"Pretty good, eh?" said Sweet Pea. She sat peacefully beside Rose as she, too, admired the view.

Far below their fairy feet were flowers of

every color and description. There were tall snapdragons, their plump yellow and red blossoms waving in the breeze. Billowing bushes of dusky lavender rustled to and fro, and ground ivy, speckled with tiny lilac flowers, crept along the moss-covered earth. Startlingly pink zinnia flowers stood proudly, while elegant yellow irises clustered along the banks of a sparkling stream.

"Where are we?" whispered Rose, noticing

that Sweet Pea's pink, peach, and lilac flowers spread down this side of the wall, too.

"Why, this is the Flower Fairies' Garden," Sweet Pea announced proudly. "It's beautiful isn't it?"

Rose nodded wordlessly.

"You'll love it here," said Sweet Pea, suddenly distracted by a floaty dandelion seed that wafted past her nose. She peered down at the dandelion clock far below. "Goodness, is that the time?" She leaped to her feet and smoothed down her pink petticoats. "I'd better be going. You take care, won't you?" she added, flinging a leg back over the wall.

"Watch out for el—" she called as she

disappeared.

'What?' Rose called after her. 'Watch out for *what?*'

But Sweet Pea had vanished.

What could she have meant? thought Rose, worry crinkling her pretty forehead for a moment. Then she shrugged—it was probably nothing.

Another dandelion seed whirled past, giving Rose a splendid idea. She flipped open her bag and tugged out Dandelion's gift, admiring the tightly packed yellow petals. It would keep her dry in the rain, but it would catch the breeze too.

"One, two, three, fly!" cried Rose. Holding her dandelion aloft and clutching her bag, she leaped from the wall and soared through the air. Slowly, gracefully, the Flower Fairy

swooped toward the garden, fluttering
her pearly pink wings occasionally to
change direction. As she approached
the ground, her feet skimmed the
topmost blossoms, releasing
delicious, flowery scents.
Lower, lower, lower she
went, until—*thud!*—she
landed on a cushion
of springy moss.
Rose sighed
with relief and
looked around.
All she could see
were flowers—no
Flower Fairies.
Where were
they?
"Well,
hello!" sang a

friendly voice. "Nice of you to drop in!" A
mischievous face popped up from behind
a bristly cornflower and skipped over. His
entire outfit—jerkin, shorts, silken slippers,
and even a crown —was pure, dazzling blue,
made from the starry petals of his flower.
"Welcome to the garden!" he added, bowing
politely and waving a regal hand. "I'm
Cornflower."

Rose clambered to her feet and bobbed a quick curtsey. "Pleased to meet you," she said, trying to ignore the warm blush that she could feel coloring her cheeks. She wasn't used to meeting strangers. "I'm Rose."

"Marvelous," said Cornflower. He looked quizzically at her, taking in the dishevelled clothes and ruffled blonde curls. "I expect you'll want to get settled in," he said helpfully, bending to pick up her bag and dandelion. "Where's your flower?"

Her heart sank. Cornflower was being so kind, so helpful, so welcoming. She didn't know how to tell him that she didn't really belong here—that she didn't have a flower, not anymore. And she didn't even know if there *were* any rosebushes in the Flower Fairies' Garden for her to make her new home. What was she to *do*?

"I'm so sorry, my dear," said Cornflower. "Here I am, yabbering away. And there you are, worn out after your journey. In fact, I bet you're so tired that you can't remember *where* your flower is." He patted her shoulder sympathetically. "I'll help you find it."

"But—" began Rose.

"No buts!" said Cornflower, flinging

Rose's bag over his shoulder and grasping
the dandelion as if it
were a floral spear. "Follow me!"

The eager fairy hopped and skipped
merrily around the garden, while Rose
hurried along in his wake. She tried once or
twice more to explain why she was there, but
it was no use. Cornflower simply said
that there was no need to thank him, and that
she should save her breath for the journey.

Eventually, Rose did as she was
told, scurrying to keep
up with the sprightly
Flower Fairy.

As they zigzagged
between the
flowers, the silent
garden seemed
magically to come
alive. Beautifully

camouflaged Flower Fairies popped out from behind blossoms, stems, and clumps of wild grass. They called out friendly greetings as the small procession passed.

Soon, Rose felt quite at home. "Everyone is *so* nice!" she exclaimed happily.

But there was no sign of a rosebush, not even a solitary rosebud. And meanwhile, the sun was moving unstoppably through the summer sky. By teatime, although they had searched most of the Flower Fairy Garden, they were still no closer to finding a place where Rose could lay her head. There remained just one place they hadn't explored.

"Why don't we try over there?" Rose asked, pointing to the dark, forbidding mass of undergrowth in the far corner of the garden.

"Oh, you won't find your rosebush in there," Cornflower said, shaking his head dismissively. "I think perhaps we'll try the area near the forget-me-nots again."

Rose hardly heard. She was far too busy pushing through the thick grasses that crowded in front of her, blocking her view.

She weaved in and out of the tall, emerald blades until eventually she emerged at the other side. There, facing her, was a terribly overgrown thicket. And poking out of the very middle of the thicket—so tiny that most Flower Fairies would have mistaken it for a sharp twig—was a thorn.

A rose thorn.

Rose grinned from ear to ear. "I've found it!" she called happily.

"A rosebush?" said Cornflower, rustling

through the grass to join her. "Really?" He
peered uncertainly at the undergrowth. "It
doesn't look very lived in," he added, looking
at Rose as if thinking that she'd quite clearly
gone mad.

"I'm sure," said Rose. "That's the place."

* * *

As the setting sun cast a rosy glow over
the garden, Rose surveyed her new home.

Cornflower had gone—reluctantly, and
with a great deal of grumbling—after she'd
persuaded him that she really would be
absolutely, totally fine and that he wasn't to
worry and that she would whistle loudly if
even the tiniest thing was wrong. But now the
light was fading fast and Rose realized that
it was getting too dark to see anything at all,
never mind explore.

She heard the gentle breathing of sleeping
Flower Fairies echoing from nearby flowers
and trees. The reassuring sound made her

feel sleepy, and her eyelids began to droop. "I *am* feeling rather tired," she murmured to herself. And using a fallen leaf as a coverlet, she snuggled down in a small grassy hollow. She soon drifted off to sleep. But her dreams were filled with strange mutterings.

Who is she? . . . I don't know! . . . What's she doing here? . . . Don't ask me! . . . Doesn't she know that we live here? . . . I don't know!

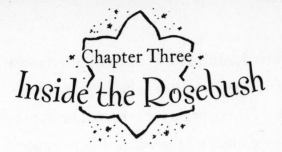

Chapter Three
Inside the Rosebush

Rose was awakened bright and early by the chirpy melody of the local lark.

"Morning!" she called out to the little bird. Then, cupping her hands around an acorn shell that had filled with dew during the night, she turned her attention to the overgrown thicket.

A dark, uninviting mass of gnarly stems reared up before her—dark and wild and spiky. Dried, crispy leaves had been blown into the bush by the wind. They plugged every gap, making it difficult to see far inside. Rose wasn't surprised that no one lived here. After thirstily draining the beechnut shell, she set to work.

First she brushed away the old, crinkled leaves. Next she carefully pruned the outermost twigs by sprinkling a touch of fairy dust onto the stems, then nipping them between her fingertips. She couldn't help pausing to admire her handiwork every few moments—the bush was looking neater and healthier already. Better still, it was starting to look like a rosebush, instead of just a heap of tangled twigs. There was still no sign of any roses though.

Then came the exciting bit. Now that she'd cleared the edge of the plant, it was time to venture inside. With small spry steps, Rose made her way to the very heart of the rosebush, pushing springy twigs and branches out of her path. It was farther than she had thought and, to make sure she didn't get lost, she left tiny sparkles of glittering fairy dust along the way. Little by little,

the light grew dim and the sounds from
the garden faded, while Rose grew more
enthusiastic with every step. She was about to
make a great discovery—she just *knew* it.

And then she did.

Suddenly, she burst through a particularly
thorny patch to find that the sun was blazing
down on the other side. And there, before
her, was the loveliest sight she'd ever laid
eyes on. In a small clearing grew a cluster of
dainty rosebushes. All were in full bloom,
their deep-red and soft pink flowers shining
like jewels against the dark green leaves.
There were tiny white rosebuds, too.

"A secret rose garden," breathed Rose. Was she the very first Flower Fairy ever to see this beautiful place? She *must* be. Otherwise, Cornflower would surely have known about it.

At once, her happiness was replaced by heartache. Rose was such a kindly soul that she couldn't bear the thought of these stunning flowers being hidden away where no one could see them. And then a thought pinged into her mind. *What if she were to clear a path through the outer bushes? Then the other Flower Fairies would be able to visit this marvelous place whenever they wanted—without having to battle their way through the spiky, dark undergrowth first.*

"Better still," she said aloud, "I could work some Flower Fairy magic on

the overgrown
rosebush too. With
a little love and
attention, it could
look as wonderful as my
secret gar—!"

A sudden squawking noise
interrupted her wonderful plan. Rose
whipped her head around to see who had
spoken, but there was not a creature in sight.
When a large, glossy crow flew overhead and
cawed loudly, she breathed a sigh of relief
and chuckled to herself. Silly Rose! She was
getting jumpy
for no reason.

Briskly she spun on her heel, ducked into
the undergrowth, and started back the way
she'd come. And as she went, she made plans.
She was going to turn her new home into a
lovely place for everyone to enjoy. And she

would only reveal the secret garden when all
the hard work was done. That way, it would
be a *real* surprise!

"Ouch!" Rose felt a sharp prickle, and her
daydream vanished. She frowned and rubbed
her leg. That wasn't supposed to happen—she
was the Rose Flower Fairy! Rose thorns
never pricked or poked her, not like they
pricked and poked the other Flower Fairies
who brushed against them. Whether it was
because she took care of roses and it was the
plants' way of saying thank you, or whether
she just had super-tough skin, Rose didn't

know. The point was . . . she didn't *feel* pointy rose thorn things.

"'Tee hee!"

Rose froze and darted quick glances to the left and right. That was no crow. It didn't sound like a Flower Fairy either. Someone was watching her—and laughing at her, too. She looked around frantically. Who could it be?

"That'll teach you to invade elf territory!" said a mocking voice.

Rose whirled to face a strange creature dressed entirely in green. He stood with his

hands planted firmly on his hips, looking rather pleased with himself.

"Who are you?" she asked bravely.

The green-clad creature gave a short laugh and clicked his fingers. Instantly, two more creatures appeared, one on either side of him. They all stared insolently at Rose, and in the brief pause that followed, she couldn't

help noticing how long and pointy their ears were. She also noticed that one of them was wielding a very sharp twig. So this was who had prodded her!

"*We*," said the leader importantly, 'are the elves. And *we* live here.'

"Pleased to meet you," said Rose. In a flash, she remembered Sweet Pea's words before she disappeared over the wall. She must have said, "Watch out for *elves*!" Rose didn't know much about elves, apart from

their reputation for naughtiness and general mischief, but she was determined not to feel nervous. "I live here, too," she added brightly. "I'm sure there's room enough for all of us."

"Ha!" barked the first elf. "But it's going to be no fun for us if you tidy everything up and

make it all light and airy and *nice*." He said
the last word as if it were a bad thing.
"*We* like it dark and tangled. *We* are the
elves."

"Yes," said Rose wearily. "You said." She
tried again, her sky blue eyes pleading with
them to understand. "The thing is, I'm Rose
and it's my job as a Flower Fairy to take care
of this neglected old plant. I've escaped from
humans and decking and concrete and patios
and *chaos* to come here. My old home is about
to be pruned, or worse."

"Chaos?" It appeared that of all Rose had
said, the bossy elf had heard just one word.
"Where is this place?" he demanded. "*We* like
chaos. *We* are th—"

"Yes, yes," said Rose hurriedly. "It's just over the wall at the edge of the Flower Fairies' Garden."

The elves' dark, beady eyes glittered. As if triggered by some unseen signal, the trio huddled together and spoke quickly in low, excited voices. Then they faced Rose. "We've decided," said the leader importantly. "You can keep your rosebush. *We're* going to make mischief."

Rose barely had time to nod before the three elves shot past her, the speed of their departure spinning her around on the spot. "Be nice to Dandelion, won't you?" she called after them.

"What do you take us for?" The indignant reply came from far away. "We're not the pixies, you know!"

Laughing with relief, Rose followed her glittering trail back through the overgrown rosebush to the outside world. Now that she'd solved the mystery of the muttering voices and said good-bye to the twig-wielding elves, she was free to get on with what she did best—tending to rosebushes.

Chapter Four
A Magical Transformation

It was hard work, but Rose loved it. Politely refusing all offers of help, she spent her days pruning and trimming and neatening up the overgrown corner of the Flower Fairies' Garden. And whenever anyone asked for a guided tour, she simply flashed them a twinkly smile and tapped her nose. "Wait and see," was all she would say. Not even Cornflower's gentle teasing could entice her to reveal more.

Each evening, when she was tired—and very happy—Rose got to know the other Flower Fairies. They were very kind, inviting her to munch on tasty mallow seeds—a special sort of fairy cheese—and brewing her fresh cups of elderberry tea. While she ate and drank, different fairies entertained her with stories from the Flower Fairy Garden. Rose hadn't realized so many charming

creatures lived there, and slowly she got to know each and every one. She was having a *marvelous* time.

The days went by. And, by the time the moon had grown from a thin, silvery sliver into a large shining ball and shrunk back to a sliver, Rose realized—with some surprise—that her work was nearly done. The overgrown corner of the garden had been utterly transformed. Gone were the long, tangled stems and withered leaves. In their place were healthy, young stems and fresh, green foliage.

Meanwhile, excitement in the garden had reached fever pitch. Although the Flower Fairies loved surprises, that didn't stop them from wondering endlessly what the hard-working fairy was up to. One day, Rose overheard two of the youngest Flower Fairies—White Clover and Heather— earnestly discussing the topic.

"I think she's practising circus tricks," said White Clover, a little fairy with round rosy cheeks. "She's learning to juggle with hazelnuts, where no one can see. That way, it's not embarrassing when she drops her nuts."

Heather wasn't convinced. "I think she's making rugs," he said knowledgeably. "She's collecting all of these old twigs so that she can weave them together. When Rose lets us inside the bush, we'll find that she's made a huge, twiggy carpet."

Rose covered her mouth to stifle a giggle, before hurrying away down the neat and tidy new path that she'd tunnelled through the rosebush. Little did the Flower Fairies know that not one but *two* surprises awaited them.

As well as tending the rosebushes, she had been busily collecting old petals to make rosewater. After collecting dew inside a large chestnut shell, Rose had added the petals to make a pink soup. Today, she was going to turn the soup into rosewater!

Carefully she climbed into the chestnut shell, which was wedged securely into a clump of moss to make sure that it didn't tip over. Lifting her left foot, then right, left, right, she squooshed and squished her toes into the water and petal mixture, turning it into a flowery mush.

"Mmmmm..." Rose sighed, as a beautiful smell began to drift upward. This rosewater would be the perfect way to thank the kind Flower Fairies for letting her stay in their garden. *Everything's ready*, she thought happily.

That evening, Rose hopped, skipped, and fluttered from flower to flower, inviting everyone to the far corner of the Flower Fairies' Garden the next day. Everyone was very excited, none more so than Cornflower, who regarded Rose as his special friend.

"Yes, yes," he said loudly to anyone who would listen. 'It's all going to be a wonderful surprise, with lots of marvelousness and fabulous splendifery. You won't believe your eyes. Just wait and see!"

Honeysuckle, who was perched high on a curling tendril, grinned broadly. "You don't have a clue what's going on, do

you?" he said, with a chuckle.

"Er ... I ... er ... well, er ... no," admitted Cornflower truthfully. "But I bet it's wonderful, all the same!"

He was right.

The next day dawned bright and clear, with not a cloud in the sapphire blue sky. Birds twittered cheerily from the branches of the silver birch tree. And the sun soon chased away the delicate wisps of mist that lingered near the ground.

Nervously smoothing down her best dress, Rose sat next to the rosebush that had once been so neglected and unloved. Now, it was a mass of green foliage. In the last day or two, tiny white-and-pink rosebuds had even begun to appear, like stars twinkling in a night sky.

Cornflower was the first to arrive. "All sorted?" he asked eagerly.

Rose nodded. There was something she needed to say—she just wasn't quite sure how to say it. Or how Cornflower would react. She took the plunge.

"The thing is, Cornflower . . . when we first met, I should have said that I didn't actually belong in the garden and that I didn't have a flower. It was just lucky that we found this rosebush—but, really, it's not mine." She didn't dare look up. "And I quite understand if you want me to leave the Flower Fairies' Garden, but I just want you to know that I love it here and—"

"Whoa there!" said Cornflower, flapping his gauzy blue wings. "Why did you think any of that would matter?" he asked, with a totally bemused expression. "We welcome all Flower Fairies into the garden, *wherever* in Flower Fairyland they come from." He raised a finger to his lips when Rose tried to speak again. "Now, not another word! This is your home now."

She smiled gratefully.

Then, one by one, more Flower Fairies

started to arrive, their faces bright with curiosity. There was Zinnia and Wild Cherry. Candytuft came next, then Lavender and Elder. Soon, everyone was there—the air buzzing with anticipation.

Rose clambered onto a toadstool so that she could see everyone. "I'd like to thank you all," she began quietly.

"Catch!" shouted Honeysuckle, throwing her one of his pinky-orange flowers. "Speak into that," he added. "Then we'll all be able to hear you!"

Rose smiled and put the trumpet-shaped flower to her lips.

"You've made me so welcome," she went on. "So I'd like to welcome you to my secret garden. Except I don't want it to be a secret anymore. I want it to be a place for Flower Fairies to enjoy."

"Hurray!" shouted Cornflower.

"You've still no idea what's going on, have you?" Honeysuckle laughed.

"Nope!" said Cornflower, shrugging his shoulders. "But it's very exciting, all the same!"

"This way," said Rose, leaping down from her toadstool and tugging aside a large leaf that she'd positioned in front of the tunnel

entrance. Then she stepped inside.

The way was leafy green and dappled with the sunlight that filtered through the rosebush. Rose had done so much pruning that the once dark and forbidding bush was light and airy. And the other Flower Fairies had no need to fear thorns—Rose had carefully twisted the stems so that the prickles pointed the other way. Ooohing and aaahing in wonder, they followed Rose deeper and deeper, until . . .

"*Wow!*" said Cornflower, as he emerged into daylight.

"*Amazing!*"

"*Unbelievable!*"

Exclamations of delight echoed around Rose's secret garden as the bedazzled Flower Fairies took

in the view. Rose had nipped and shaped
the dainty rosebushes until they were each
a perfect ball. Any wilting flowers had been
removed, leaving only the newest, freshest
blooms. The large, dark red flowers looked
as if their petals were made of velvet, while
the pale pink and white rosebuds looked like
soft marshmallows.

"And what's this?" asked Cornflower,
dunking his finger into the chestnut
shell. "Mmmm ... That smells
delicious!"

"It's rosewater," said Rose
shyly. "Dab it on your wrists
and behind your ears—you'll
smell wonderful." She
looked at the others. "It's
for everyone to try," she
said.

They didn't need

telling twice. Soon the air was filled with the beautiful aroma of roses and the sound of happy Flower Fairies as they explored the new garden.

But for Rose, the very best part of the day didn't come until much later. She was relaxing happily among the leaves of the rose garden, thinking how much she loved her brand-new home, when she heard a pattering of tiny fairy feet. She peeped round a deep red rosebud to find Clover and Heather looking back at her.

"We've got a surprise for you," said Clover proudly.

"It's a poem," Heather chipped in.

"We wrote it," added Clover.

Then, before Rose had time to say a word, they began to recite the sweetest verse that she'd ever heard.

Best and dearest flower that grows,
Perfect both to see and smell;
Words can never, never tell
Half the beauty of a rose—
Buds that open to disclose
Fold on fold of purest white,
Lovely pink, or red that glows
Deep, sweet-scented. What delight
To be Fairy of the rose.

"I can't thank you enough," Rose breathed.

"Oh, don't mention it," said Clover, suddenly bashful. 'You've given us so much loveliness, we just wanted to give something to *you*.'

Chapter Five
A Surprise Visitor

For weeks afterwards, all anyone could talk
about was the grand opening of the rose
garden. It became an even more popular
topic than the weather forecast—something
that all Flower Fairies love to talk about.
Gradually, the word spread beyond the
garden to the marshland—a wet, grassy place
that was teaming with dragonflies, minnows,
and frogs. It was also the home of the
Queen of the Meadow Fairy.
Together with Kingcup, she
ruled Flower Fairyland
firmly yet fairly. She
listened to the news of
Rose's surprise with
interest.

"I think perhaps that *I* should pay a visit to this garden," the queen mused aloud, her forehead puckered into a small frown. At once, she summoned a swallow and hopped onto its feathery back. "To the rose garden!" she commanded.

When the swallow swooped down into the middle of the inner rose garden, Rose was making herself a new party dress from pale-pink petals. She looked up in astonishment at the pretty Flower Fairy who slid gracefully to the ground. A flaxen cloud of hair framed her delicate features. She was clad in a silken ivory-colored gown, and round her neck was a necklace of large, green pearls.

"I'm the Queen of the Meadow," said the fairy. She stretched out an elegant hand and grasped Rose's trembling fingers.

"P-p-pleased to meet you," stammered Rose, frantically scouring her mind for things that she might have done wrong. Otherwise, why would the queen of the whole of Flower Fairyland have bothered to come *here*?

"I'd like to look around," said the queen, her blue eyes sweeping left and right. "Would you show me your garden?"

"Why, of c-c-course, Your Royal F-Fairyness!" said Rose. At once, she realised what must be wrong. Obviously, the queen was cross with Rose for disturbing this corner of the garden. She must have preferred it when the roses were overgrown! But there was no sign of a royal telling-off—yet. The queen simply nodded, following Rose around the sculpted rosebushes.

And that was the exact moment the three elves chose to return from their travels. Giggling to themselves, they waited until the two Flower Fairies were out of sight before randomly plucking petals from the nearest bushes and scattering them on the ground.

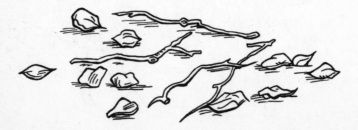

"Tee hee!" chuckled the elf in charge. "So messy!" His fellow elves nudged each other, then shook with silent laughter. When they heard voices approaching, they all hid.

"Oh!" gasped Rose, when she saw the torn petals. "I'm terribly sorry, Your Highness. The flowers are usually so neat. I don't know what happened."

The queen raised an eyebrow, but said nothing.

"I'll show you the secret tunnel," said Rose, desperate to impress the royal visitor, who she was sure must be seriously underwhelmed by now. She took Queen of the Meadow to the tunnel and led her inside.

"Pee-ew!" spluttered Rose. The tunnel smelt *awful*—as if a dozen bad eggs had been cracked there.

The queen wrinkled her nose in disapproval, but remained silent. The final straw came when she went to step back into the secret garden. A long stem suddenly shot out from the side of the tunnel, tripping her up. It was only the timely sprinkling of a little fairy dust that stopped Queen of the Meadow from sprawling on the grass.

"You can come out now," said the queen sternly, standing with her hands on her hips.

Rose popped her head out of the rosebush. "I'm sorry …" she began.

"No, not *you*," said the royal visitor tartly. Her arms were folded and she looked very cross. Suddenly, her voice softened and she pointed at three familiar figures who were now creeping out of the rosebush, their expressions sullen. "*Them.*"

"The elves!" exclaimed Rose.

"Well, what have you to say for yourselves?" said the queen, facing the mischievous trio.

The chief elf sighed dramatically. "*We* are the elves," he said petulantly. "*We* do mischief. That's our *job*."

"Then I suggest you do it somewhere else," replied Queen of the Meadow. "Rose has worked very hard to make this garden such a wonderful place. So unless you want to help with the pruning and weeding and tidying and . . ." She chuckled gaily as the elves spluttered in horror and sprinted back down the tunnel.

"*We* didn't like it here anyway!" they shouted. "It's too pretty!"

The queen turned to Rose, a wide smile

revealing pearly white teeth. "Well done," she said. "I think you've done a marvelous job. This garden is magnificent. Of course, I knew all along it would be—I just wanted to come and admire it for myself." She clicked her fingers and the swallow soared back down to the garden, landing neatly beside her.

"Oh, thank you!" said Rose.

"Farewell!" called Queen of the Meadow. "Keep up the good work!"

Rose waved until her royal visitor was just

a tiny speck in the distance. Then she settled down on a heap of moss and happily carried on with her sewing. She'd lost her old home, but now she'd found a wonderful new one and lots of fantastic Flower Fairy friends, too. Everything in her garden was truly rosy.

FLOWER
FAIRIES™
FRIENDS

Visit our Flower Fairies website at:

www.flowerfairies.com

There are lots of fun Flower Fairy games and
activities for you to play, plus you can find out more
about all your favorite fairy friends!